GRANDFATHER
MOUNTAIN

For my son, Bjorn and my grandsons, Jonas and Sylvan and in memory of my father, Jerome Newmann — B. M.

*For Grandfather Peter and our heavenly grandtwins, Felix and Oscar,
and for Anwen and Tom with love — S. B.*

Te   tén
Illu   ailey
The moral rig   d as the author
and Siân Bailey to b   ork has been asserted

First published in Great Britain in 2004 by Barefoot Books Ltd.

This book is printed on 100% acid-free paper
The illustrations were prepared in acrylics on 140lb watercolour paper

Design by Jennie Hoare, Bradford on Avon
Typeset in 14pt Bembo
Colour separation by Bright Arts, Singapore
Printed by South China Printing, Hong Kong

Hardback ISBN 1 84148 786 4

British Cataloguing-in-Publication Data:
a catalogue record for this book is available from the British Library

1 3 5 7 9 8 6 4 2

GRANDFATHER MOUNTAIN

STORIES OF GODS AND HEROES FROM MANY CULTURES

retold by
BURLEIGH MUTÉN

illustrated by
SIÂN BAILEY

Barefoot Books
Celebrating Art and Story

Contents

INTRODUCTION

Grandfather is the powerful elder who guides boys and men through the ages. He is the great teacher whose knowledge extends beyond bravery and strategy. He is the one who knows the importance of keeping the balance of nature. He is most certainly the ready warrior, and he is also the patient sage. We look to our grandfathers for their experience and for their vision, which span wider horizons and greater lengths of time than our own.

We live in an era in which gender roles are shifting. It is no longer taboo for boys and men to cry openly. It is acceptable in many parts of the world for men to raise children while women work outside the home. As we venture forth towards the unknown territory of new horizons, it is important for boys and girls and men and women to remember the wisdom and stories of their grandfathers — to know and understand the variety of male archetypes that have preceded modern times. The folktales and myths in this anthology represent eight cultures and at least eight different versions of the hero and his journey.

Grandfather Mountain begins with a retelling of the North American Seneca tale of the same name to remind us of the sacred nature of storytelling and the importance of maintaining the balance of giving when one receives a gift. As I offer this collection of stories to you, it is with a deep hope that each of you will discover the wisdom inherent in them. May the journeys of these heroes and gods guide you and inspire you as you come into your own heroic power. May these stories enrich your own growing wisdom. And ultimately, may they contribute to peace on Earth.

Burleigh Mutén
Amherst, Massachusetts 2004

'Grandfather, Grandfather, will you tell us a story?' said the children.

'Of course I will,' Grandfather replied. 'Which story shall I tell you today?'

'Tell the one about the magician who sang to the stones,' said the girl.

'No, tell the one about the warrior who killed the fish king,' said the boy.

'I want the one about the first storyteller,' said the little boy. 'Tell the one about Grandfather Mountain.'

Grandfather laughed. He put down his tools and smiled.

'I will tell you stories of gods and kings,' he said. 'I will tell you stories of magicians and heroes. I will tell you stories of great adventures and stories of love.'

The girl and the boy clambered onto Grandfather's workbench, and the little one climbed into his arms.

GRANDFATHER MOUNTAIN

NORTH AMERICA
Seneca

ONCE, LONG AGO, there was a boy named Crow whose parents both died at the same time. Crow's sorrow was so great that he built himself a shelter in the woods beyond the village. No one tried to stop Crow, for the people understood his need to be alone, and they assumed he would return when his sorrow had lessened. Three moons passed. The leaves fell from the trees, and it began to get cold. As the first snowflakes fell, Crow remembered the festival of the First Frost Moon. He thought about the songs that were sung each year at the festival. He remembered how much his mother had enjoyed those songs, and for the first time since he'd left the village, Crow longed for his home. He hastily made a bundle of his things, slung his quiver over his shoulder and began his journey back.

Now, you must realise that, during the time Crow had lived by himself, he had given no thought to his appearance. He had been busy hunting and skinning animals, gathering and storing food, making tools, clothing and shelter. He had no idea that his face and his hair were dirty. He had no idea he was in need of a bath. Unfortunately, as Crow approached his village, a group of young boys teased him, pinching their noses as they called him 'Covered-with-Filth', and then laughing and falling down on the ground.

Crow, who still felt the sorrow of his parents' death in his heart, decided on the spot to leave his village for ever. He turned on his heels and strode towards the forest without looking back. 'I'm clever and quick. I'm strong and I'm wise,' he said to himself. 'I have no need of this place.'

That night, Crow dismantled his shelter and headed south, guided by the stars. He had no idea where he was going or what he would find. As he watched the twinkling stars to keep his bearings, his

feeling of loss gradually shifted into curiosity and excitement. After some hours of walking through territory he'd never explored, Crow came upon a swiftly moving river. He followed the sound of the fast, churning current to a place where he discovered a small canoe tucked beneath the overhanging shore.

Crow looked around. Everything glistened in the moonlight. 'Thank you, Great Spirit,' he said aloud as he reached into his pouch, offering a pinch of tobacco to the river before stepping into the canoe. Crow excitedly dipped the paddle into the water and was startled as the canoe jostled back and forth beneath him. Just then, it slowly lifted out of the water and hovered there for a moment before silently rising up over the river. Crow's heart swelled with joy as he soared through the clouds into the night sky. He paddled along, still heading south as he watched the wide expanse of treetops swaying in the moonlight. He watched animals meeting at the shore of the river, and he saw the night birds and bats soaring as he sailed silently along.

At last, the canoe began to descend, slowly dropping into the river, miles from the place where it had risen.

By now, the moon was high and very bright. Moon shadows dappled the Earth, trembling as the trees swayed and rustled with the gentle breeze that swept over the river to the shore. Crow paddled quickly to shore and climbed out of the canoe. As he looked around, he immediately noticed the face of a man in the great rock cliff, which rose straight up above the river. He saw that the cliff was part of a forested mountain which was flat and open on top. 'I will build my shelter on top of this mountain,' he proclaimed. 'I will sleep next to the stars and watch the river winding and rushing below me.' Crow eagerly climbed through the forest up to the summit of the mountain. He sang softly as he cut saplings and bark for a shelter. Crow worked swiftly and accurately. Long before sunrise, he entered his shelter to lie down to rest.

Just as Crow closed his eyes, he heard the deep, raspy voice of an old man. 'Didn't you forget something, Crow?' Crow's eyes popped open like seeds bursting from their pods. His heart was pounding, but he didn't move as he strained to discern the source of this mysterious voice.

'You have journeyed far, young Crow. You are weary and excited. And you've forgotten your manners.'

Crow jumped to his feet as his hands flew to the strings of his pouch. 'Forgive me, Grandfather Mountain. You are right, I am tired, but not too tired to thank you for this beautiful place I am making my home.' Then he reached into his pouch and ceremoniously threw a pinch of tobacco over the cliff.

'Now lie down, Crow, and I will tell you a story,' said Grandfather Mountain. 'Hau'nio!'

Crow watched the stars move across the sky as he listened to Grandfather Mountain's story about the first people. When the story ended, Grandfather Mountain gave Crow some instructions. 'From now on, when I call, "Hau'nio!" signalling that I am about to tell a story, you will say, "Nio!" And as I tell the story you must say "Hey!" from time to time, so I know you are listening. When I finish the story, your gift to me will maintain the balance of giving and receiving.'

Crow at once threw another pinch of tobacco over the cliff. 'Of course I will, Grandfather,' said Crow before turning from the cliff edge and walking back to his shelter.

The next day, Crow killed several birds and many small animals. He carefully skinned them, cooked and dried the meat, and saved the skins. That night, as he waited on the edge of the cliff, he studied the stars and carved an awl from a bird's leg.

Grandfather Mountain called out, 'Hau'nio!' for a new story.

'Nio!' Crow called obediently in reply.

For many hours, Grandfather Mountain told Crow one story after another and, from time to time, Crow uttered 'Nio!' and 'Hey!'

just as he'd been instructed, always throwing a pinch of tobacco over the cliff to express his gratitude for each story. When the last story was told, Crow decided to give Grandfather Mountain the awl he had just made. 'Here, Grandfather, is something I made with my hands.'

The next day, Crow discovered a village far to the east of the cliff. Some of the hunters offered to show him how to hunt big animals, and within a week he had killed his first deer. Crow was pleased to make himself a fine suit of clothing. Then, feeling the need for a fancy pouch, he asked the hunters for the name of the most talented quill stitcher in the village. On their advice, he approached the shelter of an old woman. To Crow's amazement, the old woman's granddaughter greeted him with a beautiful pouch she had decorated with glistening beads in the shape of a crow.

'As you can see, I have been expecting you, Crow,' said the maiden. 'Here is your pouch.'

The grandmother stepped forward and smiled, taking Crow's hands in her own as she looked into his eyes. 'I saw you in a dream, young Crow. I saw you coming this way to marry my grandchild. Two moons have passed, and we have been busy preparing for your arrival. Welcome, Crow.'

Crow looked at the maiden, and he couldn't help smiling. His heart was full of gratitude and love. A feast was prepared, and Crow married the girl at dawn.

Crow and his bride moved to Crow's lodge on the cliff. The first time Grandfather Mountain called out, 'Hau'nio!' Crow's bride smiled. 'This is the voice of my own grandfather,' she said. 'It is a great gift to hear his voice and his wisdom again. Now as we listen, you will carve an object to represent each story, and I will make you a pouch to carry them in.'

As winter passed, Crow and his bride eagerly listened to many stories of the sky people in the world up above and the first people on Earth, of the animals, the land, the sun and moon. By spring, Crow's story pouch bulged with stories.

One day, Crow's wife suggested that they travel north. 'Let's visit the people of your village,' she said, smiling.

'I couldn't do that,' replied Crow, feeling his heart swell with sadness. 'I turned my back on my village without saying goodbye to anyone.'

'Never mind,' replied his wife. 'You are the carrier of the stories now. Grandfather gave you the stories so you can carry them to the people. Now you will be greeted with respect wherever you go. It's time to go north,' she insisted, looking up at the darkening sky.

Crow's wife led the way down the cliff right to the place by the river where Crow had hidden the canoe. 'You know about this canoe?' Crow asked, confused. His wife laughed. 'Who do you think sent this magical boat to you?' she replied. Crow smiled as he and his

wife climbed into the canoe, which again lifted out of the water as soon as he dipped the paddle into the river. Again, it silently soared through the clouds and past the stars.

When they descended, landing close to Crow's village, his wife told him to disrobe. 'Take off your clothes and walk through this tree,' she suggested, pointing to a magnificent hollow elm. By now, Crow had no doubt in his wife's wisdom, so he willingly entered the huge, hollow tree and emerged wearing a special suit of clothing, decorated with intricate embroidered patterns, and similarly beaded moccasins.

As they walked into his village, no one recognised Crow. First the children and then all the adults of the village surrounded the dignified pair. Crow greeted his people respectfully. 'I am the orphaned boy, Crow, who left this village full of sorrow and anger many moons ago. Now I return to tell you of my journey and to give you the stories I received from Grandfather Mountain.'

The people looked from Crow to each other. 'Stories? What stories are these?' they asked one another.

'Gather round,' invited Crow, reaching into his story pouch. 'I will tell you the story of the sky people in the world up above. I will tell you the story of the first people on Earth, and of the animals, the land, the moon and the sun.'

Crow pulled one story object out of his pouch after another. 'Hau'nio!' he cried with great delight as he started each story, smiling as he heard the people reply, 'Nio!' Crow saw the people's eyes widen as his stories surprised them. Their laughter rang in his ears when his

15

stories filled them with joy. Crow began to understand the power of storytelling as he watched the people's faces changing from joy to sadness to fear and back to joy. He began to understand the importance of the stories and of his position as storyteller.

As soon as Crow returned home to the mountain, he walked directly to the edge of the cliff where he had heard so many stories. 'Hau'nio!' he cried, reaching into his pouch. Crow lifted his hands above his head in a sacred way, and he threw a pinch of tobacco in each of the four directions.

'Nio!' answered Grandfather Mountain.

'Some moons ago,' said Crow, 'there was a lonely orphan who magically found himself standing on Grandfather Mountain's shoulders. This boy, who is now a man, was given great gifts by this grandfather. I will honour you, Grandfather, for the rest of my days. I will tell the stories of the sky people and the first people. I will tell the stories of the animals, the land, the moon and sun. Just as you honoured me, I will honour you, Grandfather, by giving what I have received.'

Crow kept his word. He told stories to the people until he was a very old man. But before Crow died, he made sure that his grandson knew all the stories in the pouch. And when Crow's grandson was a very old man, he made sure that his grandson knew every story in the pouch. In this way, grandfather to grandson, the stories were passed down through the generations to you.

ORUNMILA MEETS ESHU ON THE ROAD

NIGERIA
Yoruba

LONG, LONG AGO, one very hot morning, Orunmila thrust his
spade into the soil so it stood up by itself, and he wiped his brow.
He had been digging yams in his garden since the first light of dawn.
Orunmila took a long, slow drink of water from his gourd, and he
looked out over his garden to the trees that were as still as stone. No
wind was stirring, but with the speed of a tornado, a thought rushed
into Orunmila's mind. In that instant, he saw the crowded streets of
Owo. He smelled the fragrant spices in the market, and he proclaimed,
'Enough gardening under this hot-bellied sun! I am off to Owo!
Why, I cannot remember the last time I saw that city!' He pulled his
spade out of the soil and carried it to his hut. 'Today is the day I go
to Owo,' he announced.

Orunmila walked straight to the ornately painted wooden box
that he kept on a shelf in his hut, and he gently put it down on the
floor. Squatting in front of the box, he sang a short prayer and slowly
lifted its lid. Orunmila reached his long, slender fingers into the box
and then, one by one, removed sixteen shiny white cowrie shells,
which he carefully placed on the floor in the shape of an oval. He
slowly held his hands over the shells and began swirling them in two
great circles. With one swift swoop, Orunmila scooped up all the
shells, cupping them between his hands. He quickly brought his
hands to his mouth and whispered secret words to the shells.

'What lies ahead on the road to Owo?' he asked. Then Orunmila
threw the shells on to the dry earth. As the soft dust settled around
the shells, Orunmila's high forehead creased into eight deep furrows.
He folded his arms over his chest. There was no mistaking that the

shells would not give him any information. 'He who asks for guidance will get none,' was the message.

Orunmila scratched his head and sighed. Then he quickly scooped up the shells again, cupped them in his hands and shook them for quite a long while before he threw them on to the earth again. As the dust settled, Orunmila sprang to his feet as if the shells were about to bite him. 'Not even your father can say what will happen on this journey,' he read.

'Ha!' said Orunmila to himself as he scooped up the shells and put them back into the box. 'Thank you very much, little friends,' he said. 'I like a mystery. Your silence will not stop me from having fun today.' He carefully placed the shells in the box, quietly closed the lid and put it back on the shelf. He grabbed his walking stick, slung his water bag over his shoulder and began his journey to Owo.

Orunmila stood tall and strode happily along on the one wide path that led to Owo. As the sun began to set on the first day of his journey, Orunmila spied his brother, Eshu, walking towards him, obviously coming from the city of his destination. The two gods smiled and nodded to each other, passing one another without saying a word.

Now, Orunmila should have stopped right there. First the shells gave no information about his journey, and now he met Eshu, God of Chance and Unpredictability, on the path to Owo. Orunmila certainly knew that Eshu often appears as a warning when an accident is about to occur, but he was already having too much fun to stop and think. He happily strode on towards Owo.

The next day, as the sun began to set in the late afternoon, Orunmila again spied his brother, Eshu, on the road, coming towards him from the city of Owo. 'Could it be?' he wondered. 'Could the brother who passed me yesterday, pass me again today, coming from the same place?' He smiled nervously at Eshu, who was smiling at him, and they nodded to each other.

Although Orunmila hadn't spoken out loud, Eshu looked straight into Orunmila's eyes and answered his thoughts. 'Yes, I am once again coming from Owo.'

Now this time, Orunmila did stop for a moment. He considered the peculiarity of two men going in opposite directions passing each other on the same path two days in a row. But then, remembering his destination, he took a deep breath and lengthened his gait. With determination and excitement, Orunmila strode on towards Owo.

On the third day of Orunmila's journey, when he saw Eshu walking towards him again, Orunmila began to worry. Even so, he would not stop. He looked at Eshu, nodded, and quickly looked away as he kept right on walking.

On the fourth day, Eshu waited for Orunmila near the gate to Owo. As he saw Orunmila approaching, Eshu laid some fresh kola fruits on the path and walked towards Orunmila. The two gods nodded to each other, and Orunmila couldn't help asking, 'Eshu, are you once again coming from Owo?'

'Why do you doubt what you see?' asked Eshu. 'Of course, of course. What you see is what you get.'

Orunmila felt his stomach tighten. His forehead creased into eight deep furrows.

'Something is definitely peculiar,' he said to himself, but he was so close to Owo, he couldn't consider turning round. After a few steps, however, he did stop, turning to look over his shoulder. He saw Eshu looking at him. 'Maybe I should consult the palm nuts,' he thought as he touched the pouch that hung from his waist. 'No need,' he decided. 'I am almost there.'

Orunmila nearly tripped over the kola fruits that Eshu had left on the path. 'What good luck,' he remarked as he picked them up and began to devour them.

'Thief! Thief!' called out a farmer from Owo, who came running towards Orunmila with his knife in his hand. 'That kola fruit came from my garden! Thief! Thief!'

The farmer attacked Orunmila, who yelled in his own defence, 'I found these fruits on the path. I never saw your kola tree, wherever it is. I am not a thief!' But the farmer was too angry to hear a word Orunmila said. As Orunmila fought off the farmer, the farmer's knife cut the palm of Orunmila's hand. He finally broke away from the farmer and ran back down the path towards home.

22

As soon as Orunmila was out of the farmer's sight, he collapsed into the bushes by the side of the road. 'I've never stolen anything in my life,' he said indignantly to himself, 'but now the people of Owo will think I'm a kola fruit thief.' Confused and exhausted, Orunmila soon fell asleep.

Eshu saw the whole skirmish between Orunmila and the farmer. That night, as his brother snored in the bushes beside the path, Eshu quickly entered the city of Owo. As he whisked through each hut, Eshu cut the palm of each sleeping citizen, including the honourable Oba of Owo. Then he returned to the gate of the city, and Eshu cut the palm of his own hand.

As sunlight began to stream across the sky on the fifth day of Orunmila's journey, he rose early and returned to the path, striding towards Owo. There, by the city gate, sat Eshu.

'Eshu, it is obvious that you are setting obstacles in my way,' proclaimed Orunmila. 'We are brothers and we are friends. Why are you making this journey so difficult for me?'

'We are good friends,' said Eshu. 'Continue your journey. The city of Owo awaits you. Let's go together, and if there is trouble, I will speak on your behalf.'

The two gods strode into the city side by side, and as soon as the farmer saw Orunmila, he hurried to the Oba, demanding that Orunmila be punished for stealing his kola fruits. A crowd surrounded the gods, and the people of Owo, who were not used to strangers, began to whisper, 'Kola fruit thief! Punish the thief, punish him now!'

Eshu stepped forward as soon as the Oba arrived and spoke on behalf of his brother. 'This man strides into your city a stranger in the bright morning light with nothing to hide, and you welcome his good intentions with accusations and threats of punishment. What proof do you have that he is a thief?'

'Look at his hand,' insisted the farmer. 'I cut the palm of his hand with my knife as we struggled on the path yesterday.'

The Oba turned towards Orunmila. 'Show your hands, sir,' he demanded. 'If you are innocent, your palm will be healthy and whole. If your palm is wounded, we will all see your guilt.'

Eshu took a step forward again and spoke to the Oba. 'Why is this man who strode into your city in the bright morning light asked to show his hands when no one else in Owo has been asked to show their hands? Any man here could have stolen the kola fruits of this farmer.'

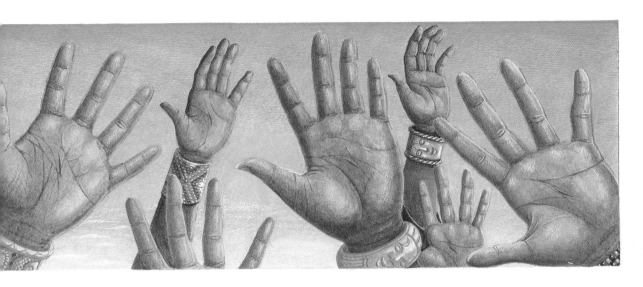

The Oba looked at the farmer. He looked at Orunmila and Eshu.
Then he nodded and demanded that all citizens hold up their hands.
They did so and saw that each one of them, even the Oba and Eshu,
as well as the farmer, had a fresh wound on their palms. Amazement
and confusion spread through the crowd, quickly turning into loud
pandemonium.

Eshu struck his staff on the ground to quieten the crowd. 'If a cut
on the palm is the sign of a thief, then we are all thieves,' he
announced.

The Oba sighed and proclaimed Orunmila's innocence. 'We have
made a mistake. We have greeted this stranger with false accusations.
Bring him gifts to show our regret. Bring him gifts to welcome this
stranger to Owo.'

'You are right to treat us well,' said Orunmila. 'I am the first son
of Olodumare, and this is my brother, Eshu.' A low utterance of

surprise came from the crowd as the people of Owo ran to bring gifts of fruits and nuts of all kinds to the gods. A feast was made on the spot. The Oba thanked Eshu and Orunmila for teaching him how to deal with unexpected visitors to his city.

'That was a close call, my friend,' whispered Orunmila to Eshu. 'Thank you for saving my name in the city of Owo. The shells and the sight of you walking towards me each day on the path should have told me to be careful. I won't ignore the wisdom of the shells again. Nor will I ignore you.'

'Glad to hear it,' said Eshu. 'Let's enjoy the feast.'

THE SONS OF RANGI AND PAPA-TU-A-NUKU

NEW ZEALAND
Maori

IN THE BEGINNING, there was only the night. During that lonely, dark time, Rangi the Sky thought he sensed someone somewhere below him. He looked through the never-ending blackness and finally he spied Papa-tu-a-nuku the Earth, rotating through space far below him. Rangi was so happy to see someone else in that vast field of darkness, he immediately lowered himself and hovered directly above her. Papa-tu-a-nuku trembled with excitement. She had been longing for someone to love. Papa-tu-a-nuku opened her arms and held Rangi close to her for a very long time. They were happier than they had ever imagined, so they kept on hugging and kissing.

Soon Papa-tu-a-nuku gave birth to six strong sons. And still she and Rangi would not stop hugging and kissing each other. 'I love you more than life itself,' Papa-tu-a-nuku whispered into Rangi's ear.

'I will kiss you and hug you for ever,' replied Rangi. 'I never want to be alone again.'

After quite a long time, their sons, who were gods, became tired of standing around in the dark, being ignored by their parents.

'It's time to get on with things,' said Tane, God of the Forests and All Things that Live in the Forests. 'I've got work to do, and I can't see a thing. I need some light and I need it now!' he cried. 'Father, you need to leave Mother to make room for the sun and the moon and the stars. We need light to do our work, which we can't even begin by just standing around in the dark like this!'

Rangi did not answer his son. He kept right on kissing and hugging his Papa-tu-a-nuku.

'We'll have to pull them apart,' declared Tane.

'I've got a plan,' said Tu, God of War. 'Father will have no one to hug if we kill Papa-tu-a-nuku. I have plenty of arrows and spears.'

'Don't be ridiculous,' replied Tane. 'We can't kill our mother. She is the Earth! She is the ground we are standing on. There will be no work at all if she is not here.'

Tu coughed. 'I know that,' he replied. 'Without her, nothing will exist, not even us. But if we are ever to get on with our work, there must be light. Somehow we must pull those two apart.'

The brothers agreed, except for Tawhiri, God of Winds and Storms. 'Look at our parents,' said Tawhiri. 'You can see how much they love

29

each other. How can you think of breaking them apart? I won't have anything to do with your plan to separate them,' he said, turning his back on his brothers. Rongo-ma, God of Cultivated Food, finally spoke. 'We are gods, waiting to rule this world. I need light to plant my garden, and light can only be born when the Sky returns to the heavens. Rangi is clinging to Papa-tu-a-nuku and she is clinging to him. We have to separate them. I will be first to try!' Rongo-ma grabbed hold of Rangi's feet and pulled. He pushed and he pulled until great streams of perspiration rolled off his forehead. Gasping for breath, he fell over. 'Who will try next?' he implored.

Tangaroa, God of the Sea and All Things that Live in the Sea, puffed out his chest with his great fists resting on his hips. 'I will,' he proclaimed. Tangaroa straightened his back and stretched to his full height, flexing the muscles in his big arms. Then he leaned his shoulder against Rangi and pushed and shoved until he also fell down, exhausted.

'My turn!' said Haumia, God of Wild Growing Food. Haumia walked some distance away from Rangi and Papa-tu-a-nuku, turned and began running towards the determined parents. Haumia hit them with a thud, and he, too, fell down exhausted. Rangi and Papa-tu-a-nuku had no intention of letting go of each other. They were as close as ever.

30

'Now who is ridiculous?' said Tu. He pulled in three deep breaths as he raised his hands over his head, striking Papa-tu-a-nuku and Rangi again and again. With each blow, Rangi and Papa-tu-a-nuku tightened their grip on each other more fiercely. Tu, God of War, was unable to separate the Sky from the Earth.

Tane, God of Forests, shook his head. He paced back and forth with his hands behind his back as he thought for a very long time. Then he walked over to Rangi and Papa-tu-a-nuku. He placed his head next to his parents' sides, and pressed against them. Slowly, ever so slowly, he gradually pushed his head and then his shoulder in between Rangi and Papa-tu-a-nuku. Grunting and groaning, he finally let out a great roar as he pushed his whole torso and his own two legs between the Earth and Sky. The five brothers could barely see Tane, he was so squashed between the two parents.

Then Tane pressed both of his shoulders against his father's body, and he pushed both of his feet against his mother's body. Rangi and Papa-tu-a-nuku moaned in pain. 'Why are you doing this?' they demanded. 'Why are you prying us apart?' Papa-tu-a-nuku held on to Rangi, and Rangi held on to Papa-tu-a-nuku, but Tane did not stop pushing. His body trembled as his torso turned into a tremendous, thick kauri tree. Quivering and groaning, Tane slowly, ever so slowly, pushed his father, the Sky, back into the heavens.

Just as the gods had predicted, sunlight flashed over everything as soon as Sky and Earth were separated. The golden moon soared into the night sky, and the stars began to twinkle like bright white diamonds. Birds of all kinds and insects took flight, and the deer and gazelle shot across the Earth with grace and speed. The gods were astounded by the beauty of all that had just been born.

Tu, Rongo-ma, Tangaroa and Haumia let out great cheers. 'Bravo, brother! Now there is light! Now there is day and night! Life will flourish on Earth!' All four of them shouted. 'Bravo! Bravo!'

Tawhiri did not cheer. He scowled at his brothers, and he followed Rangi through the clouds up into the heavens. 'Father, this was not my idea,' said Tawhiri. 'I will avenge my brothers for what they have done.'

Rangi's sorrow and longing for Papa-tu-a-nuku were so great his wide shoulders shook as he cried. Great rushing rivers of tears flooded the Earth. Small pools of water quickly turned into large lakes all over Earth's body. 'Smite those brothers of yours!' he commanded.

Tawhiri nodded. He sucked in a huge gust of wind that roared through his throat, filling his lungs with air. Then he leaned forward

and blew great growling storm clouds and howling fierce winds through Tane's magnificent forests. The tallest and strongest trees were pulled up by the roots and crashed down. The gods clung to their mother as she trembled with fear.

Tawhiri sped over the oceans, blowing Tangaroa's great waters into towering waves that lifted the sea up on to the land. Whales and dolphins, sharks and eels and many fish died, shivering on the shore. Tawhiri flew over the land, pounding against Rongo-ma and Haumia's lush green fields with all of his might, so that every berry bush and vine, every fern and sweet potato were destroyed. Tawhiri looked around and smiled. He was proud of his strength.

Lastly, Tawhiri turned towards Tu, God of War. Now Tu climbed on to the mountain above his mother's heart. He anchored his feet and leaned back into the vast rock wall behind him. 'I'll take care of this bully, Mother,' he called out. 'This nonsense is almost over.'

Tawhiri roared and charged against Tu again and again, but Tu was invincible. Tawhiri at last collapsed defeated, but he didn't care. He had avenged his father, the Sky. A stillness finally fell over the Earth.

33

Papa-tu-a-nuku smiled at Tu. 'When the God of War creates peace, I have to laugh,' she said. Then she picked up Tawhiri. 'Your brothers were right, my son. In order for this world to be born, your father and I had to be split apart. Now let's clean up this mess.' Then she gave all the songs of power to Tu, who in turn gave them to his brothers. He taught Tane the songs to reseed the forests. He taught Rongo-ma and Haumia the songs to enhance green-growing plants.

He taught Tangaroa the chant for calm waters. And he even taught Tawhiri the chant for mild breezes and gentle zephyrs.

The six brothers worked together, and eventually Earth's creatures enjoyed the beauty and peace of her waters and land. One day, Tane took some red clay in his hands, and he made the first woman. He mated with her and, in time, the first woman gave birth to a daughter who, in time, also gave birth to many daughters and sons. Tane's family was the first family of humans.

From the day Rangi returned to the heavens, the sun's light warmed and lit Earth. Many plants and trees grew and flourished, and the humans worked hard. At night, when the moon and stars sent their delicate light down to Earth, the humans rested, knowing that another day would follow.

Rangi never stopped loving Papa-tu-a-nuku. Nor did she ever stop loving him. They continued to gaze longingly at one another, remembering when they were young and had held each other close. Rangi still misses his great love, the Earth, and it is said that his tears are the gentle dew that moistens the grass during the night.

QUETZALCOATL CREATES THE FIRST PEOPLE

MEXICO
Aztec

LONG AGO, in the time before time, a great flood covered the Earth, destroying all life on the planet. After the rains had stopped and the water receded, the gods and goddesses gathered on a mountain to survey the damage.

'Earth is still beautiful,' said Star Skirt.

'The land is still covered with lush green trees,' said Milky Way, 'and the sun still shines on the sea.'

The Bridger turned to the rest of the gods and said, 'Now is the time for Earth to be populated with humans.' Everyone nodded in agreement.

'But who,' asked the Tiller, 'will collect the bones of the ancestors to create the humans?' The gods looked at Quetzalcoatl, whose bravery

was known to them all. 'You are the only one who can find the
bones in the Land of the Dead, Quetzalcoatl,' said Star Skirt. 'Will
you collect the bones?'

Quetzalcoatl adjusted his hat and cleared his throat. 'Of course,' he
replied. Then he pointed his sparkling staff towards the Land of the
Dead as a gust of wind lifted him into the air. Quetzalcoatl soared
over the lands and seas and swooped down to the lowest valley on
Earth to the entrance of the Land of the Dead.

'Who goes there?' bellowed the Lord of the Dead.

'I am Quetzalcoatl. I have come for the precious bones of my father.'

'The bones of your father? What are you planning to do with
those old bones, Quetzalcoatl?' demanded the Lord.

'Now that the flood has subsided, we want to populate the Earth with humans,' replied Quetzalcoatl.

'Ah,' replied the Lord of the Dead, stroking his chin. 'If I give these old bones to Quetzalcoatl so he can make humans,' he thought, 'this will be good for me. Eventually these humans will die, and they will become my servants. I like this idea.' The Lord of the Dead smiled and said, 'I will give you the bones, Quetzalcoatl. Yes, you may have the bones of your father, but first you must blow the conch in all four corners of the Land of the Dead.'

'That's only fair,' said Quetzalcoatl. 'I will blow the conch in all four corners of this dark place.'

Then the Lord of the Dead handed Quetzalcoatl a large, smooth conch. Quetzalcoatl thanked him and immediately set off to find the first corner of the Land of the Dead. When he reached the first corner, he excitedly lifted the conch to his lips and blew. All that was heard was the gust of Quetzalcoatl's breath rushing against the inside of the shell. 'How is this possible?' he asked himself, examining the shell. It had no holes. No air could pass through it.

Quetzalcoatl laughed to himself. 'The old Lord of the Dead has a sense of humour,' he thought. 'Okay, I will show him who I am.' Then he called for the large and small worms who crawl in the Land of the Dead to burrow four holes in the conch. He called for the large and small bees who sleep in the Land of the Dead to awaken and enter the conch. The worms worked quickly and opened four holes in the rim of the shell. The bees zoomed inside the conch and buzzed so loudly the shell shook in Quetzalcoatl's hands. Again he lifted the conch to his lips and blew. The buzzing of the bees roared through the shell like the great winds of a hurricane, trumpeting throughout the Land of the Dead.

'What power!' said the Lord of the Dead. 'This Quetzalcoatl is a clever god.' Then he waited, and sure enough, after some time, the Lord of the Dead heard the conch trumpet again as Quetzalcoatl reached the second corner. When the Lord of the Dead heard the conch blast in the third and fourth corners, he called for the bones of Quetzalcoatl's father.

'Take them,' he said to Quetzalcoatl, handing him the brittle, white skeleton of his father. But as soon as Quetzalcoatl turned his back, the Lord of the Dead changed his mind. He couldn't bear to give up those precious bones, so the Lord of the Dead instructed his servants quickly to dig a deep, wide pit in the tunnel which leads to Earth's surface. Quetzalcoatl was so awestruck by the bones of his father, he did not see the pit. Just as he got to its edge, four quails flew out of the pit, flapping and screeching, startling Quetzalcoatl. He stumbled and fell into the great hole, dropping the bones, which scattered and broke into pieces.

When the Lord of the Dead heard the clatter, he laughed, assuming that Quetzalcoatl was dead. After a long while of lying perfectly still, Quetzalcoatl opened one eye. Without making a sound, he placed all the precious shards of bone into his hat, climbed out of the pit, and carefully made his way to Earth's surface. As soon as he stepped out

39

into the light of day, Quetzalcoatl flew straight to Serpent Woman.

'Here are the bones of my dear, dead father, such as they are, in pieces,' he said. 'Can they still be used to make humans?' he asked, embarrassed because he had dropped them.

Serpent Woman smiled. 'Of course, of course,' she said, 'but the humans will not all be the same size. The little pieces will make short people and the larger pieces will make tall ones. Some will be fat and some will be thin. There's nothing I can do about that.'

'Good enough,' replied Quetzalcoatl as he watched Serpent Woman grind the bones into a flour-like powder. When she had finished, she carefully swept the bonemeal into a large jade bowl with her jewelled hand-broom.

Quetzalcoatl took the bowl of bonemeal to the gods. The Tiller, the Bridger, the Emerger and the Shooter each blessed the bonemeal with a drop of their blood and, sure enough, the new race of humans was born.

'Look at them. Aren't they adorable?' said Star Skirt. 'They are hungry. These dear little humans need food.'

'What will they eat?' asked Milky Way.

'Who knows what will suit them?' asked the Bridger.

'Where will we find food for these humans?' asked the Tiller.

'I will look for their food,' said Quetzalcoatl. 'I will find something for them to eat.'

Quetzalcoatl began the search. After some time, he felt tired, and he sat down on a boulder. It was so hot he fanned his face with his hat. As Quetzalcoatl placed the hat down on the rock, he noticed a tiny red ant carrying a kernel of maize. 'Hello, little beast,' he said. 'What are you carrying? Could this be food, my friend?'

The ant pretended she didn't hear Quetzalcoatl. She didn't want to tell him about the great food source she had found. Quetzalcoatl gently picked up the small creature. 'Do you notice how much larger I am than you, little friend?' he asked. 'Do you notice my staff and my hat? Do you know who I am?'

'I am not uninformed,' answered the ant. 'I know you are the glorious God of Sun and Wind. I know you have created the human race. And I am humbly aware of how large you are and of how small I am.' She paused and then sighed. 'This delightful object I am carrying is maize. Yes, maize is food. I will show you the source of this food. Gladly, I will show you where it is found.'

So Quetzalcoatl turned himself into a tiny black ant. And he followed the red ant into a stony mountain, squeezing through one opening after another until at last they entered a vast chamber full of maize, seeds and beans of all kinds. There were enormous piles of red, yellow, white and blue maize and huge piles of beans and seeds — all filling the place that would soon be known as Food Mountain.

'Fantastic!' said Quetzalcoatl. 'Now I just need to move this mountain closer to the humans.'

Quetzalcoatl ran as quickly as his little ant legs could carry him out of the mountain and immediately resumed his human form. He shoved and he pushed against Food Mountain. At last he had to admit that he hadn't budged it one inch. Quetzalcoatl called for the Emerger, the Bridger, the Tiller and the Shooter, who all put their shoulders against the mountain, but it still would not move.

'Ask the ants to carry out the food for the humans,' suggested the Bridger.

'They're too small,' said Quetzalcoatl. 'That would take for ever.' He was so frustrated, he stamped his foot and struck the mountain with his staff. To everyone's surprise, the mountain split open and kernels of maize, beans and seeds streamed out. Quetzalcoatl laughed and lifted his staff, stirring up a wind that scattered the seeds, beans and maize in all directions.

Star Skirt and Milky Way ground the maize into a nourishing meal and put it on the lips of the infant humans. The humans liked the sweetness of the maize. They quickly grew into strong adults, and they planted more maize. The first humans gave birth to more humans, who worshipped the gods who had given them life and food.

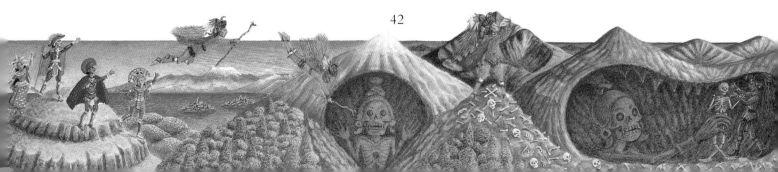

ASCLEPIUS: HEALER OF THE ANCIENT WORLD

GREECE

LONG AGO, when Zeus ruled Heaven and Earth, his favourite son, Apollo, fathered a son with a mortal maiden. The child, Asclepius, was born on the side of a mountain, where he was left in the care of two goddesses disguised as a black dog and a she-goat. As the dog and the goat waited for Apollo to come for his son, a kindly young shepherd discovered the baby swaddled between the animals. Fearing for the tiny child's safety, the shepherd hurried to pick him up. Just as he bent over the child, the baby smiled and began to glow with a golden light that instantly surrounded him in a large, brilliant halo.

'Oh ho!' said the shepherd, backing away. 'A baby god, are you?'

And he left the child right where he lay. That night in the village, the shepherd heard stories of a healer being born who could cure any illness and even raise the dead. The innocent shepherd had no idea that the divine baby he had stumbled upon would grow up to be Asclepius, the greatest healer of the ancient world.

Apollo found his son on the mountain and carried the child directly to the wise old centaur, Chiron, who took one look at the baby and exclaimed, 'This is a special boy, Apollo! Leave him with me, and I will raise him well. I will teach Asclepius everything I

know.' Since Chiron was an esteemed healer, skilled in the arts of medicine and surgery, Apollo agreed to allow the old man to foster his son.

By his sixth year, young Asclepius knew all the medicinal plants by name, as well as the basics of human anatomy. He knew where each plant thrived — in forest or field, in sunshine or shade. He knew the names of each bone in the body and all of the organs. 'You are a special boy, Asclepius,' said kindly old Chiron. 'Yours will be no ordinary life.'

When Asclepius was eight, Chiron put him in charge of the pharmacy. When he was ten, Chiron asked him to assist with surgery. When he was thirteen, Asclepius performed his first surgery alone, saving the life of a man whose heart had stopped beating. He began

to have dreams about his patients, dreams about the source of their illnesses, dreams about the appropriate cure. Word travelled quickly about the boy healer. Now people began to travel from afar to be treated by both the old man and his student, Asclepius.

Zeus looked down to Earth from Mount Olympus. He saw the crowd of people waiting to see Asclepius. 'I see that your son is attracting a lot of attention,' he said to Apollo. 'No one has ever healed as many people as Asclepius has.'

'That's my boy,' said Apollo, puffing up his chest as he strutted back and forth in front of Zeus.

'That's my grandson,' boasted Zeus, puffing up his chest as he elbowed Apollo out of his way. 'Don't you think a boy with power like that needs a proper temple for his healing work? The ill and injured are flocking to see him.'

Apollo arranged for a temple to be built on the mountain where Asclepius was born. A series of forty columns supported its wooden roof. Beneath the black marble floor a gurgling stream fed into a fountain. At one end of the temple were sculpted images of the gods, and at the other end, in honour of Chiron, were images of the centaurs. An enormous ivory and gold statue of Asclepius was placed in the temple. His dog was at his feet.

'This is very grand, Father,' said Asclepius.

'As is suited for the son of a god,' replied Apollo. 'You are the grandson of Zeus; it's only fitting.'

'And you have always been a special boy,' said Chiron.

'A temple in my honour is one thing, said Asclepius, but if it isn't too much to ask, a stadium would be more useful so the ill and injured could strengthen their bodies with exercise.'

'Of course, of course, right away. Whatever you say — you're the healer,' said Apollo, dispatching orders for a very large stadium. 'What else do you need? What else does my brilliant son need?'

'Theatre,' replied Asclepius, scratching his head. 'Theatre is healing for the infirm. Music, dance and story are relaxing and instructive. An amphitheatre, if you don't mind, on the side of the mountain.'

'Yes, yes, of course,' said Apollo. 'No problem. Anything else?'

Asclepius asked for temples to honour his elders — Zeus, his grandfather, and Poseidon, his great-uncle, as well as for his favourite aunts, Artemis, Hecate, Aphrodite and Themis. On the top of the mountain, close to the sun, Apollo had a temple built for himself.

After Asclepius's patients had bathed and dressed in white robes, they slept in a special dream temple. In the morning, they told their dreams to one of Asclepius's priests, who then explained the cure that was needed. Once a blind boy dreamed he had found a lost dog. The priest immediately led the boy to Asclepius's dog, which licked the boy's eyes, restoring his sight. A man whose hand was paralysed dreamed he was throwing a ball. In the morning, the priest took him to the stadium where Asclepius held the man's hand until his fingers began to move.

One moonless night, Artemis, Goddess of the Hunt, arrived while everyone slept. She touched Asclepius's shoulder to wake him.

'What's this?' he asked. 'A visit from my adventurous aunt!'

'Hush,' whispered Artemis. 'Something horrible has happened. My own brother, Apollo, your father, tricked me into mistakenly pointing my arrow at my dear friend Orion. Of course, I pierced him through the heart. I never miss my mark,' she moaned. 'Look,' she cried, pointing to the body on the floor. 'Here he lies, lifeless.' Then she burst into tears of grief and regret.

Asclepius kneeled down to examine Orion's body. The great hunter was indeed dead. As Asclepius looked up at Artemis, he saw her pull a vial out of the pouch she wore on her chest. 'This is the blood of a gorgon,' she whispered. 'You can bring Orion back to life with this blood. You can do this, Asclepius. Only you have the power to do it. I beg you, take pity on my error and bring my dear friend back to life.'

Asclepius examined the vial of blood. He knew the stories about the great gorgon's power to revive the dead. He stared at the corpse and then at his aunt. 'I am special,' he thought to himself. 'Everyone says it. Why not attempt the impossible?' Then he nodded, whispering, 'I will do it. I will do it for you, but this is our secret, Aunt.'

News about Orion's untimely death reached Zeus quickly. He watched Artemis steal her way to Asclepius's side in the dark of night. 'Who does Asclepius think he is? I am the only one who can revive the dead! Farewell to your glory, Grandson!' roared Zeus as he watched Asclepius open the vial over the corpse. Then, grabbing one of his thunderbolts, Zeus hurled it into the heart of Asclepius. Just before it reached its mark, Orion lifted his head. The bolt tore through Asclepius, who collapsed on the floor.

Without Asclepius's power, Orion fell back into death.

Apollo's heart swelled with grief when he heard this news. His grief turned quickly to rage as he realised his illustrious son was gone for ever. Shaking with fury, Apollo flew to the cave of the cyclops who forged Zeus's weapons. 'No mercy for you!' he screamed as he slew the smith. Zeus was furious with his son. He nearly killed Apollo. But, after all, Apollo was his favourite son, so instead Zeus punished him with a year of hard labour — tending sheep.

Artemis pleaded with Zeus to revive Asclepius. 'I begged him to do this unthinkable thing. It's not his fault,' she implored.

Zeus shook his head. 'He who uses his gift unwisely will lose it,' he replied.

'At least,' cried Artemis, 'place Asclepius and Orion in the heavens, for my sake. If it weren't for me, neither one of them would be dead.'

Zeus took pity on Artemis and nodded. He raised his hands and lifted Asclepius and Orion into the heavens. If you look into the night sky, you can still see them: Asclepius and his serpent and Orion with his bow.

MERLIN AND THE GIANTS' RING

ENGLAND

L ONG, LONG AGO, there was a lively young boy and a very old man who were friends. Merlin, the old man, was the most famous bard in the land. He could see the future as clearly as the present, and his ability to weave a spell with words and song set him apart from all magicians of his day. Merlin's young friend was Arthur, who would some day be king, although he did not know it then.

One evening, as Merlin and Arthur were walking at dusk, Arthur looked up at the old wizard and asked, 'Would it bother you terribly to tell me once again the story of...'

'...the Giants' Ring?' Merlin finished, chuckling. He stretched his long arms up towards the sky. 'You are in luck. The wind blows from the east, and the evening star is gleaming above the horns of the bull.

It's a fine moment to retell that tale.'

Arthur looked out towards the bright star that appeared like a twinkling eye over the wide, sly smile of the crescent moon. He wondered if it really mattered whether the moon was aligned with the star or where the wind came from.

'Start with Vortigen!' he demanded, skipping around Merlin. 'Don't leave that wicked old ruffian out of the telling, please.'

'Hmm,' said Merlin, as he pulled an ancient grey conch from his sleeve and blew three shrill blasts to start the story. 'Did I ever tell you that Vortigen, that devious upstart, crowned himself? Vortigen didn't have the courage to challenge the High King to combat, so he poisoned his stew. By the time most of the country knew what had happened, Vortigen had hidden himself in his castle up north. No one knew where he was, but I saw him inside my eyes. I saw him wringing his hands, barely sleeping all through the night, terrified of what would happen next, terrified of his own death.

'Vortigen's counsellors had heard about me. The boy wizard, they called me. Even Vortigen had heard of my visions, so he dispatched his soldiers to fetch me at once.

'I'd seen an image of them, jostling in their saddles, as I gazed at the fire the night before they arrived. I was ready to mount when they got to our gate. As I climbed on to my horse, Mother rushed out from the house to place my father's blue cloak over my shoulders.

'You remember, Arthur, that I never knew my father, don't you?'

Arthur leaned forward. 'Yes, of course I do,' he replied. 'What about Vortigen? Tell me about Vortigen,' Arthur pleaded as he hunched his back, weaving the fingers of one hand through the fingers of the other, imitating the ruffian, King Vortigen.

'Yes, yes,' Merlin laughed. 'That is exactly what Vortigen did when he saw me. He couldn't hold his troubled hands in his lap, as hard as he tried. I entertained the whole hall full of nobles with songs and stories, and then a hush came over the place as Vortigen narrowed his eyes, and leaned towards me, hissing, "Can you see your king's death? Can you do that, my boy?"

'I stared into his eyes, and I adjusted my father's cloak so it rested on my back. I placed my hand over my heart, and finally I spoke: "I am bound, my lord, to speak of the future since danger is near. I am bound to tell all that I see because, at this very moment, the floor of the forest trembles beneath the thundering hoofs of an army heading this way. Within hours, Aurelius and Uther, the sons of our former king, will take your life and your throne. You, my lord, will die gasping for air."

'Vortigen's eyes narrowed into tiny slits as I told the truth. With each word, he leaned closer and closer to me, and as soon as I had finished, he leaped up, grasping for my throat. I stepped back as he roared, "How dare you threaten your king! You are the one who will die gasping for air!"'

Arthur jumped to his feet, he was so excited with the telling. 'And then you disappeared! Right before the king's eyes!' he cried 'Poof! Like a wisp of smoke!'

'Yes, yes,' said Merlin, 'but do let me finish. Yes, I disappeared. And before dawn,

Aurelius and Uther's army had surrounded the castle. Their flaming spears soared over its walls, driving Vortigen to the tower, where he soon choked on great billowing clouds of black smoke. Aurelius took the throne and restored peace in the kingdom.'

'Hooray!' cried Arthur, jumping up and down. 'Then you set up the Giants' Ring to honour the soldiers who died fighting against Vortigen!'

Merlin nodded and sat down on a log to rest. 'You are skipping ahead in the story, Arthur. If it wouldn't bother you terribly, could you once again hold your tongue a while and listen to the tale?' Arthur lowered his eyes and nodded.

'First, King Aurelius was told by his counsellors about my knowledge of spirit and the power of my sight. He took me to the great battlefield on Salisbury Plain where many brave men have died through the ages. He told me of his plan to erect a colossal monument to honour the dead. As King Aurelius named all the great battles and all the great men who had fought on the plain, I heard a chorus of their cries, the clanging of metal against metal, the thud of men falling, and the deep, slow moaning of death. I felt a great, aching sorrow fill my chest, and I began to feel the soil sink slightly beneath my feet. Along with all the other sharp sounds in my head, there was a slow, rhythmic keening that I immediately recognised as the voice of Mother Earth herself.

"This noble place needs healing," I thought to myself. And I instantly asked the king to dispatch six ships and an army of his strongest men to Mount Killarus in Ireland to dismantle the Giants' Ring and reassemble it right there on Salisbury Plain.

"'Ho, ho," laughed King Aurelius. "What are you saying, Merlin? Don't we have enough stone right here in Britain to build a proper monument? Isn't our stone good enough to honour our dead?"

"'My lord, do not laugh at what you do not understand," I replied. "It's the particular vibration created by the ancient stones that will honour those who died bravely. When the Giants brought the stones over the sea and placed them in a circle within a circle, they knew what they were doing. Each stone has its own magic, and arranged as they are, they create a massive energy field that is like medicine. If I may say, sir, this battlefield is crying out for healing. The Giants' Ring will stand as a testimony to you, a king who properly honours the dead. It will stand as testimony to the lost lives of Britain's soldiers. And it will bring a profound healing to this blood-soaked place. Not to mention that it will stand for ever."

'Aurelius stroked his beard. Then he turned to Uther, immediately
commanding him to assemble an army and a fleet of ships. Within
two days, we were on the high seas with a steady, strong wind that I
conjured myself, speeding us straight to the Irish shore. A small Irish
army engaged us there in a tenacious fight, which quickly resulted in
their speedy retreat, and Uther commanded the army to begin
dismantling the Giants' Ring.

'The soldiers slowly circled the gigantic stones, not speaking a
word. Anyone could tell that the Ring held an ancient secret power.
Anyone with any common sense would be scared to dismantle this
holy structure. And then, of course, there was the problem of how to
dismantle something so huge. The immense, grey stones towered
over us like giants, daring anyone to try to uproot them.

'Uther's plan was to dismantle the outer ring first, so the soldiers
dug a deep trench all around the base of one of the outer stones.
Then fifty men, shoulder to shoulder, leaned together into the huge
stone, attempting to push it down. They moaned and they groaned.
Sweat dampened their hair and poured over their faces, but the stone

didn't move an inch. Then they built two gigantic ladders which they propped against the stone, heaving great, thick ropes around it, and they tried to pull the great slab down. Again, they moaned and groaned, giving all their strength to the task. Just before dusk, they flopped flat on the ground, full of frustration…'

'…and exhaustion!' cried Arthur, as he threw himself to the ground like one of the men in Uther's army.

'Exactly,' said Merlin, going right on with the story without looking at Arthur. '"How about a little help, Merlin?" Uther called out to me. "You're the magician!"

'"Yes, I am, sir," I replied, striding into the middle of the inner ring. I placed a crystal in the centre of the altar stone, which sat like a great plate waiting for my offering. Then I waited with my arms at my sides for the moon fully to crest the horizon. As its light stretched over the land, hitting the stones, vast shadows were cast over the place, and I began to walk in and out of the shadows in the double swan pattern, first towards the east and then towards the west. I sang as I wove in and out of those giant stones and the great moon shadows they cast, first in the softest voice I could manage and then in the loudest voice I could manage. I knew the men were wondering what I was saying. I was wondering what I was saying!'

'It was the Giants' language!' insisted Arthur.

'Perhaps,' replied Merlin. 'I worked all through the night, walking and singing, walking and speaking, back and forth among the stones in the patterns I knew, and when the sun suddenly sprayed golden-red

light all over the place, I called to each stone by name. One by one, like a row of dominoes, each huge slab slowly tipped over and fell to the ground, jarring the men off their feet as they trembled with awe.

'Uther's soldiers loaded the stones on to the ships, and we quickly sailed home. The men laboured quickly, following my directions, to dig the precise pattern of the Ring. Then they dragged the monstrous slabs to the plain and laid them all out in proper order. During the evening of the following full moon, I walked from dusk to dawn singing and speaking in that odd, old language as I went in and out of shadow in the double swan pattern. As the first light of day reached the Ring, I called each stone again by its name. One by one, each giant slowly rose so it stood like a huge, rigid soldier over me, until all the stones were in place.

'Aurelius and Uther were delighted by the majesty of the Ring. Together they bowed before me. I was glad to honour the dead, and I was glad to serve the king, but it was the soft, humming voice of Mother Earth beneath my feet that pleased me the most.'

Arthur dropped to the earth, stretched out on his belly and put his ear to the ground. 'I can hear her! She's still humming!' he cried.

BRAVE-AND-SWIFT-
IMPETUOUS-ONE
SLAYS THE SERPENT

JAPAN
Shinto

LONG AGO, when Brave-and-Swift-Impetuous-One left the heavens for ever, he descended to the head waters of the River Hi. There he sat for a long time, watching three streams flow into one wide river. He gazed at the trembling water rippling in long, curved rows like delicate dancers moving with ease. Brave-and-Swift-Impetuous-One had never been to Earth. 'This is where I belong,' he said softly, remembering that his father had given him the Earth to rule over when he was born. Brave-and-Swift-Impetuous-One stroked his eightfold beard. He sighed deeply, remembering his family in heaven.

'What's this?' he asked as he spied a small stick floating from the middle stream into the wide river. Brave-and-Swift-Impetuous-One

61

did not take his eyes from the stick for a moment. He smiled as it quickly floated towards him. Leaning out over the bank, he grabbed it and cried, 'A chopstick! There are people nearby! There are people upstream!' Brave-and-Swift-Impetuous-One sprang to his feet, clutching the chopstick in his hand as if it were a jewelled sceptre. He strode towards the middle stream, quickly breaking into a loping run as he hurried towards the source of his discovery.

It wasn't long before Brave-and-Swift-Impetuous-One was at the foot of a mountain where he found the humble home of an old man and woman. 'Ahh!' they both said, recognising the god and bowing before him. 'Welcome, Great One,' said the man. 'Please honour us by being our guest for tea. I am He-Who-Heals-With-His-Feet, and this is my humble wife, She-Who-Heals-With-Her-Hands.'

Brave-and-Swift-Impetuous-One accepted the invitation without hesitation. He chattered on and on about how he had discovered the chopstick, describing in great detail how he had leaned over the rushing water to catch it and how he'd sped his way alongside the middle stream to their home. Brave-and-Swift-Impetuous-One was so busy talking that he didn't notice the deep lines of worry and sadness that marked the faces of his host and hostess until She-Who-Heals-With-Her-Hands began to pour tea. Then he saw a thin stream of tears slip out of her eye. He looked at He-Who-Heals-With-His-Feet and saw that his eyes were also brimming with sorrow.

62

'What troubles you, Old Ones?' he asked. 'I am strong, I am fast, and I am clever. Surely I can help you with any problem, whatever it may be.' Brave-and-Swift-Impetuous-One eagerly asked again, 'What is it that troubles you so?'

'If you please, let us introduce our daughter,' replied He-Who-Heals-With-His-Feet, clapping his hands twice. A graceful young woman immediately appeared at the door of the house and bowed to her parents and their esteemed guest. 'This is our precious daughter, Wondrous Princess,' said the old man. Brave-and-Swift-Impetuous-One's eyes opened wide. He stared at the sleek, shining hair of Wondrous Princess, which glistened like the darkest night reflected on water. He stared at her deep, black eyes and her angular cheekbones. Then he remembered his manners and bowed to show his respect.

She-Who-Heals-With-Her-Hands smiled as she wiped the stream of tears that continued to flow over her cheeks. 'This is our only daughter,' she said. 'This is our precious Wondrous Princess.' And then her tears flowed like a river and her shoulders shook with sorrow, making it impossible for her to speak.

'Once we had eight lovely daughters,' said He-Who-Heals-With-His-Feet. 'Eight daughters, all as lovely as Wondrous Princess, who is now our last living child.'

63

'What happened to your children?' asked Brave-and-Swift-Impetuous-One. He-Who-Heals-With-His-Feet looked quickly at his wife and daughter as he nodded. The two women immediately covered their ears and closed their eyes.

'Royal One,' whispered the old man, wringing his hands, 'each of our daughters was devoured by the mighty serpent, Eight Forks, who drags himself across the land every year at this time looking for prey.'

Brave-and-Swift-Impetuous-One's heartbeat quickened. He was intrigued by the opportunity to meet such a beast. 'Please, if you will, Old One, tell me what Eight Forks looks like,' he asked.

'Eight Forks' body spreads the length of eight hills and eight valleys,' replied the old man. 'The eyes on all eight of his heads bulge like overripe winter cherries. Thick, blackish-green moss spreads over his back upon which tall trees sway as he slithers along, moaning and groaning, scraping and bruising his belly.'

Brave-and-Swift-Impetuous-One's eyes clouded over. For a moment, he stared into the western sky. Then he bowed to the old couple. 'With all proper respect, with your best interest at heart, will you entrust your daughter to me for her own protection?'

'With all proper respect and all of our gratitude, of course we will,' replied the old couple together.

Brave-and-Swift-Impetuous-One smiled at Wondrous Princess and said in a barely audible whisper, 'You need not be afraid ever again.' Then he turned her into a delicate ivory comb in the shape of a rising sun. Placing it securely in his royal bun, Brave-and-Swift-Impetuous-One turned towards the old man and asked, 'Do you know how to brew rice beer?'

'Of course,' replied He-Who-Heals-With-His-Feet.

'Then follow my instructions precisely,' said the god. 'Every time the beer has brewed, add water and malt again, so that each time the brew becomes stronger. Do this eight times, and when the beer is ready, construct a long red fence in the shape of a circle. Build eight wide gates in the fence and at each gate build a sizable platform. On each of the platforms place a good-sized vat of the eightfold beer. And when you have done all of this, stand next to me, and we will wait.'

He-Who-Heals-With-His-Feet and She-Who-Heals-With-Her-Hands scurried like mice storing seeds as they brewed the beer and made the fence. In short order, the eightfold rice beer and the circular red fence with eight gates, eight platforms and eight vats were ready. She-Who-Heals-With-Her-Hands poured the beer into the vats without spilling a drop, and the old ones joined Brave-and-Swift-Impetuous-One on their porch to wait for the serpent to appear. Just as the old man had predicted, they soon heard the beast groaning as it slithered over rocks and trees, bruising its great bulging belly. They heard it sigh and chortle as it rounded the mountain, coming into view of the house.

Eight Forks lifted himself up as he spied the unusual red structure with eight gates, each holding a vat of the potent beer. His eight tongues darted out at once, and he immediately slid over to the enclosure. Lowering his heads towards the vats, he sucked in the eight-fold beer and let out a roaring belch that passed through the area like a hot, odious wind. Moaning and groaning, Eight Forks slowly pulled himself into a huge, perfect coil within the fence. Then, one by one, he yawned with his eight mouths as his heads dropped to the Earth with a thud that shook the ground beneath the old couple's house. Within minutes, Eight Forks was snoring a slow, rhythmic roar.

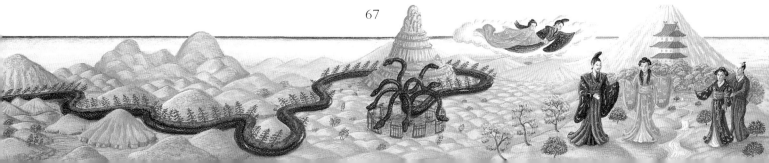

Brave-and-Swift-Impetuous-One jumped off the porch, bolted towards the enclosure and leaped over the red fence. He unsheathed his gleaming sword and held it high over his head eight times, each time lowering it into the body of the drunken serpent. Eight great rivers of blood flowed into the River Hi, which was soon as red as the evening sky.

'You need never be afraid again,' proclaimed Brave-and-Swift-Impetuous-One as he bowed to the old couple. Then he carefully removed the comb from his hair, which instantly turned back into Wondrous Princess.

'We are safe!' claimed her parents, whose smiles were as wide as the horizon. Wondrous Princess bowed to Brave-and-Swift-Impetuous-One. 'You — Esteemed One — have restored my parents' joy. To you I will always be faithful.'

Brave-and-Swift-Impetuous-One bowed to Wondrous Princess. Then he took her hands in his and began to ascend into the air. Together they soared above the trees as Brave-and-Swift-Impetuous-One looked for a proper place to build his palace. When the spot was chosen and the palace was built, he married Wondrous Princess and appointed her father the master of his temple.

THE *W*AR BETWEEN THE GIANTS

IRELAND
Celtic

I N THE TIME BEFORE TIME, a family of half-fish, half-human sea folk took to living on land. These giants, who had one leg, one arm and three rows of teeth, were called the Fomors. Although they liked living on land, the Fomors had to return to the sea on a regular basis to replenish their strength. Several centuries passed peacefully for them until one blustery day when the North Wind swept a vast cloud over the land.

The cloud appeared to be caught on the top of the tallest mountain, where it blew in the wind like a huge, billowy blanket for days. Then one morning the cloud disappeared, revealing a large group of giants making their way down the mountain.

The Tuathans were handsome to look at, with two legs, two arms,

and one set of teeth. They were gifted and clever, having come from a place where the magical arts are common knowledge. They wore colourful clothing and played harps and flutes and sang with voices that sounded like birds.

Balor, the Fomor king, summoned his generals to gather their troops at the foot of the mountain. As soon as the last Tuathan had descended, Balor hopped forwards and struck his spear against the ground. 'I am Balor, beware!' he roared, pointing to his left eye, which he kept closed. 'When I open this eye, it will kill all that I see!' he bellowed. 'Fear for your lives, strangers! I am king of the Fomors, and now I am your king as well.'

Every Tuathan turned to look at their leader, the Dagda. He smiled and adjusted the belt around his plump belly. Then he held up his palms to show that he carried no weapon. 'This fish-head who calls himself king has no manners,' thought the Dagda to himself. 'No manners, blunt weapons and a deadly eye — if he tells the truth.'

'King Balor, we come in peace to this place,' said the Dagda. 'Will you please join us for a feast? Let's eat and talk and explore our opinions.'

'Yes, let's eat,' agreed Balor who was always hungry.

The Dagda laughed and his big belly shook as he served everyone from his cauldron, which constantly replenished itself. 'Shared food is the answer to many disputes,' he said again and again. When he finally sat down with Balor, the Dagda proposed that the two races — the Fomors and the Tuathans — rule over the land together.

'While you Fomors replenish yourselves in the sea, we'll take care of the land and protect it from future invaders,' he suggested. Balor was impressed with the Dagda's thinking as well as his bottomless cauldron. And when the Fomors had eaten all they could eat, Balor agreed to co-rule with the Dagda.

The Dagda's daughter, Brigit, married Balor's son, Bress, under a brilliant blue sky on the longest day of the year. The Dagda's fingers flew over the strings of his harp, and his magical music turned the leaves on all the trees gold, yellow, orange and red. He played on, and the colourful leaves turned brittle and dry, floating to the ground. Then the air suddenly turned cool and got colder as the music called forth snowflakes that swirled through the air. The Dagda laughed loudly as everyone danced, and gradually he brought back the warm winds of spring. Everyone cheered as blossoms burst open to celebrate the partnership of the two races.

All went well for a while, until Balor's son, Bress, became king. Bress taxed the Tuathans for having hearths in their homes. He taxed their gold and took the milk of their cows and all of their meat. The Tuathans lived under the constant threat of Balor's evil eye, and the Dagda himself was put to work building forts and castles.

'Appear to be joyful no matter what happens,' the Dagda advised his people. 'The day will come seven years from now when we will drive the one-leggeds back into the sea, too terrified ever to return.'

Nearly seven years later, on a moonless night, Bress led an army of soldiers out of the sea, declaring war on the Tuathans. As soon as the Dagda heard the news, he sent forth his druids to utter magical words against Bress's army. Several miles away, Bress abruptly halted, yawning as he said to his commander-in-chief, 'I don't know why, but I'm suddenly overcome with exhaustion. Set up camp for the night, and we'll rest right here.'

Since the Tuathan army wasn't ready for battle, the Dagda decided to stall for some time by paying a visit to Bress. When he got to the Fomor camp, Bress was in such a deep sleep that he couldn't be roused. His commander-in-chief offered the Dagda some porridge, knowing how fond he was of good food. The Dagda accepted the offer and sat down to eat, but before he lifted his spoon, the commander-in-chief proclaimed that if the Dagda didn't eat all of the porridge, which filled a vat the size of a house, he'd be killed on the spot.

'If it tastes as good as it smells,' said the Dagda, 'there will be no problem.'

Indeed, the Dagda ate every last spoonful of porridge, although his belly rumbled and trembled as if it were about to explode when he rose from the table. He heard the Fomors laughing as he waddled away, moaning and groaning, thinking to himself, 'The joke is on you, you fish-heads.'

Now the Tuathan army was ready, and they waited while Bress slept off the druids' spell. When he finally awoke, Bress was astounded by the numbers of Tuathans who were already gathered on the battlefield.

The first battle was an enthusiastic match of equals. The Fomors lost about as many warriors as the Tuathans. But as the days wore on, and individual duels left hundreds dead on the battlefield, the Fomor army and its weapon supply began to dwindle, while the Tuathans never seemed to run out of shining, new weapons. Tuathan soldiers who had fallen on the battlefield one day seemed to appear the next, hearty and fit, eager for battle. 'Send a spy to their camp to see what is going on,' Bress ordered.

The spy, disguised as a Tuathan warrior, strode into the Tuathan camp. He made his way directly to the weaponry forge, where the smith grabbed hold of his dented sword and his lance. 'So your weapons need some sharpening, eh?' the smith said as he held the sword and lance over the fire, clanging them together twice, rendering them clean and sharp, gleaming like new. The spy's eyes widened. He had never seen magic like this. 'Watch this,' said the smith, pushing a rod of hot metal into the fire and mumbling magic words.

A moment later, he pulled out a glistening spear lighter in weight and sharper than any metal weapon the spy had ever seen.

The spy reported all that he'd witnessed to Bress, who instantly sent him back to the forge to kill the smith. Sensing that he was doomed, the loyal spy followed his king's orders. He asked the smith for a new lance, and immediately thrust it into the unsuspecting man's chest. Roaring with rage, the smith pulled it out of his body and threw it into the spy, killing him on the spot. The smith staggered to the Spring of Health, where he immersed himself in its magical waters, instantly healing his wound.

The Fomors eventually discovered the spring, and soon had filled it with stones. Without its miraculous healing powers, the Tuathans were at a disadvantage. Feeling victorious, Bress rallied his soldiers, providing each of them with a new coat of mail, a plumed helmet and a strong sword.

All the Dagda's great warriors were assembled for this battle. Just before dawn, commander-in-chief Lugh strode through the Tuathan soldiers, encouraging them to fight for the glory of independence. 'It's better to die fighting for freedom than to live as a slave to these fish-folk,' he said. 'We will be victors today!' he proclaimed, and all the men cheered.

Lugh was loved and respected by everyone. His smile made everyone smile, and when he was excited, his face glowed like the rising sun. Long, bright rays of light shot out for miles around.

'What's that?' demanded Bress from across the plain, seeing a bright light on the western horizon behind the Tuathan camp. 'The sun is rising in the west? What sort of omen is this?'

'That's not the sun, sir,' replied one of his men. 'That is the face of Lugh, the Dagda's chief warrior.'

Bress wondered what sort of warrior glowed like the sun, and he let out a yell, ordering his army to charge just as the Dagda raised and lowered his huge arm, signalling the Tuathans to do the same.

The earth shook as the two armies of giants ran across the plain, swords flashing and clanging when they met. The soldiers roared like lions. Arrows, spears and javelins flew through the air in such numbers they looked like a great storm of lightning bolts zinging across the plain. Metal scraped against metal, squealing and screeching. One giant after another crashed to the ground, wounded and dying, soaking the earth red with death. Commanders of both armies were slain, including the Tuathan smith and many generals. Bress himself met his death. More men died that day than there are stars in the sky.

Old Balor, who survived, finally found himself face to face with Lugh. 'Lift up my eyelid!' growled the old king to his men.

'Yes, lift it up, Balor!' cried Lugh. 'Open the Gate to Death!' he called as he slid his sword into its sheath at his waist.

Five Fomor men quickly attached a hook to Balor's great drooping eyelid and began cranking it up to expose the deadly evil eye. Lugh smiled and pulled a gleaming piece of quartz out of his pouch along with his slingshot. He set the quartz in the sling and took aim. Lugh

waited until he could see the crest of the upper part of the eye rising like the sun, and then, just as the pupil began to appear, he let his missile fly. The quartz flew straight through Balor's eye socket, piercing through his brain and the back of his head, pushing the evil eye right through, instantly killing him. The evil eye shook the ground as it landed at the feet of Balor's commanders, whose shock overpowered their reason. They stared dumbstruck at the deadly eye and dropped to the ground, instantly killed by the old king's gaze.

Now there were very few Fomors left and no leaders, so the defeated sea folk rushed into the sea, never to return, just as the Dagda had predicted. For many ages, the Tuathans enjoyed the beauty and bounty of Ireland. The Dagda ushered in each season with his magical harp and blessed the crops, feasting with everyone from his bottomless cauldron.

Eventually, another race of people — the human beings — came to Ireland. Guided by the Dagda's wisdom, the Tuathans cast a veil of invisibility over themselves. 'We are happy here,' the Dagda pronounced. 'Here we will stay. From this day forth, we will be visible only to those who are pure of heart. Only those who can see beneath the surface will know about us.' Then the entire Tuathan race reduced themselves to the size of tiny mice, and to this day, they are known as the fairy folk.

Grandfather could tell by their bright eyes that the girl and the boy were eager for more stories.

'I have told you all the stories I know,' he said, smiling. 'And look at the little one. He is fast asleep. I must take him to bed.'

'Yes,' said the girl. 'He fell asleep right after he heard the first story!'

'I'll make sure I tell him the one about the eight-headed serpent,' said the boy.

'And I'll tell him the one about the harp that changes the seasons,' said the girl.

Grandfather laughed. 'You are good listeners. You will be good storytellers too.'

Sources

Adlington, Richard and Delano Ames, (tr.), *Larousse Encyclopedia of Mythology,* Paul Hamlyn, London, 1959.

Alpers, Antony, *Maori Myths & Tribal Legends*, John Murray, London, 1964.

Austin, Alfredo Lopez, *The Rabbit on the Face of the Moon*, University of Utah Press, Salt Lake City, Utah, 1996.

Baldwin, Neil, *Legends of the Plumed Serpent*, Public Affairs, New York,1998.

Bett, Henry, *English Myths and Traditions*, B. T. Batsford, London, New York,Toronto, Sydney, 1952.

Brundage, Burr Cartwright, *The Fifth Sun: Aztec Gods, Aztec World*, University of Texas Press, Austin and London, 1979.

Carlyon, Richard, *A Guide to the Gods*, William Morrow, New York, 1981.

Chippendale, Christopher, *Stonehenge Complete*, Thames and Hudson, New York, 1983.

Courlander, Harold, *A Treasury of African Folklore*, Crown Publishers, Inc., New York, 1975.

Curley, Michael J., *Geoffrey of Monmouth*, Twayne Publishers, New York, 1994.

Fraulich, Michel, *Myths of Ancient Mexico*, University of Oklahoma Press, Norman and London, 1997.

Graves, Robert, *The Greek Myths*, Penguin Books, London and New York, 1955, 1960.

Ions, Veronica, *Indian Mythology*, Paul Hamlyn, London, 1967.

Jayne, Walter, *The Healing Gods*, Yale University Press, New Haven, 1925.

MacColloch, J. A., *The Religion of the Ancient Celts*, Constable, London,1911.

Monmouth, Geoffrey of. Lewis Thorpe (tr.), *The History of the Kings of England*, Penguin, London and New York, 1966.

Morgan, Lewis Henry, *League of the Iroquois*, The Citadel Press, Secaucus, New Jersey, 1975.

Parker, Arthur, *Seneca Myths and Folk Tales*, University of Nebraska Press, Lincoln and London, 1989.

Parrinder, Geoffrey, *African Mythology*, Perter Bedrick Books, New York,1976.

Radice, Betty, (ed.), *Hindu Myths*, Penguin Books, New York, 1982.

Reed, A. W., *Treasury of Maori Folklore*, A. H. & A. W. Reed., Wellington, Auckland, Sydney, 1963.

Rees, Alwyn and Brinley, *Celtic Heritage*, Thames & Hudson, London,1961.

Rolleston, T. W., *Myths and Legends of the Celtic Race*, Farrar & Rinehart Publishers, New York, 1936.

Séjourné, Laurette, *Burning Water: Thought and Religion in Ancient Mexico*, Thames and Hudson, London, New York, 1957.

Squire, Charles, *Celtic Myth and Legend Poetry and Romance*, Newcastle Publishing Company, New York, 1975.

Taube, Karl, *Aztec and Maya Myths*, British Museum Press, in cooperation with University of Texas Press, Austin, 1993.

Thomas, P., Epics, *Myths and Legends of India,* D. B. Taraporevala Sons & Company, Bombay, 1961.

Walton, Alice, Ph.D., *The Cult of Asclepius*, Cornell Studies in Classical Philology, Ginn & Company, 1894.

Barefoot Books
Celebrating Art and Story

At Barefoot Books, we celebrate art and story with books that open the hearts and minds of children from all walks of life, inspiring them to read deeper, search further, and explore their own creative gifts. Taking our inspiration from many different cultures, we focus on themes that encourage independence of spirit, enthusiasm for learning, and acceptance of other traditions. Thoughtfully prepared by writers, artists and storytellers from all over the world, our products combine the best of the present with the best of the past to educate our children as the caretakers of tomorrow.

www.barefootbooks.com